Dragon Eggs Book 5

Dragon's Song

Emily Martha Sorensen

Also by Emily Martha Sorensen

Wicked Witches of Restva:
Black Magic Academy

Fairy Senses:
Fairy Eyeglasses
Fairy Compass
Fairy Earmuffs
Fairy Barometer
Fairy Pox
Fairy Slippers
Fairy Lunchbox
Fairy Icepack
Fairy Stopwatch
Fairy Toothbrush
Fairy Perfume

Dragon Eggs:
Dragon's Egg
Dragon's Hope
Dragon's First Christmas
Dragon's Fire

Comics:
A Magical Roommate
To Prevent World Peace

Picture Books:
Tabby, Tabby, Burning Bright

The End in the Beginning:
The Keeper and the Rulership
The Fires of the Rulership
The Magic or the Rulership

Trilogy of a Teenage Werevulture:
Trials of a Teenage Werevulture
Trifles of a Teenage Werevulture
Weredodo Sleuth

The Numbers Just Keep
Getting Bigger:
Twenty-Four Potential
Children of Prophecy

Not Quite a Harem:
Not Quite a Curse

Magical Mayhem:
To Prevent World Peace
To Prevent Chic Costumes
To Prevent Clear Paths
To Prevent Smart Choices
To Prevent Warm Welcomes
To Prevent Cute Mascots
To Prevent First Place (prologue)

Short Story Collections:
Worlds of Wonder
Magic and Mischief

Dragon Eggs Book #5: Dragon's Song
Copyright © 2018 by Emily Martha Sorensen
Cover art by Eva Urbaníková

ISBN-13: 978-1722689209
ISBN-10: 172268920X

http://www.emilymarthasorensen.com

To Liz,

who has done a lot of urgent,
last-minute beta-reading for me,
even when it was personally inconvenient.

Thank you for that.

Thank you also for that whole
"being a great sister" thing.
That makes it really nice to be around you.

CHAPTER 1
Sums

The newest dragon egg was now in a cage beside Violet's. Rose eyed the silent egg as her son and the other *Deinonychus antirrhopus* child played together, leaping on top of each other and biting each other's tails.

A telepathic squabble broke out between the two.

Violet's tail looked like prey! Virgil would pounce on it!

Violet's tail was *not* prey! She was scared of Virgil's pouncing! She would smack him in the face with it!

Whack!

Rose chuckled. It was amazing just how easily those two could be entertained by the simplest of games. She supposed she shouldn't be surprised; they were only five months old and three months old, after all.

Whack! Virgil would hit Violet in the face with his tail, too!

Wham! Violet liked playing tail face!

Thwack! Virgil liked playing tail face, too!

As the two merrily continued their game, Rose found her mind and her eyes wandering over to the mysterious silent egg.

You woke up a few weeks ago, she thought, *but unlike the other three who have awakened so far, you did not bond with a parent immediately, nor even seem that interested in doing so. Who are you? What sort of person are you?*

It was a question Rose had wondered many times while in the presence of the egg, but, as always, there was no response. The tiny female in the egg had woken up once while Rose had been here, but she had left behind only a feathery impression of hunger before her consciousness had drifted off again.

Which was another fascinating question Rose badly wanted the answer to: Did dragons in the egg feel hunger? Theoretically they shouldn't, since they should have all of the nutrients they needed until hatching, but Virgil had made vague references to hunger a few times while in the egg, which seemed to imply that eggbound fetuses might be familiar with the sensation.

Then again, those references from him might have only been an echo of his ancestors' memories. Such secondhand experiences might have taught him to remember how the sensation felt, even if he had not yet experienced it personally.

That was one thing that was deeply confusing about raising a member of a telepathic species. Sometimes she wondered how much he had learned by himself, and how much he had learned from his ancestors' memories.

She hoped there weren't essential pieces of knowledge that *Deinonychus antirrhopus* society had led parents to hide from their very young children until they were older.

She hoped he wasn't missing core memories that would be necessary for him developmentally.

There were no adults left of his species. There were only a few hundred eggs scattered across the country, and it wasn't even guaranteed that all of them would hatch in the same generation. While Virgil could pluck Rose's memories out of her head, whether or not she wanted him to, that did not mean she'd have all the knowledge he would need as he grew into adulthood.

There was a feathery impression of stirring, and a wispy impression of hunger. Rose's head turned immediately to the egg in the cage beside Violet's, but nothing more happened.

She sighed.

A terrible scream shrieked from Violet's cage.

Virgil had bitten Violet's tail! Violet was very sad! Violet's tail hurt! Violet's tail had been bitten!

Rose spun around in intense frustration. "Virgil! No biting!"

But Violet's tail had looked like prey. Virgil wanted to hunt prey. Virgil would pounce again!

Violet let out another blood-curdling shriek.

"Virgil!" Rose shouted. "Stop it!"

Virgil sulked and drew back. His mother was thinking that if he didn't stop, he'd have to go home right now. His mother was mean. He wanted to play tail face again.

"Yes," Rose said with annoyance. "Tail face is fine."

Virgil would hit Violet in the face with his tail! Virgil was hitting Violet in the face with his tail! Virgil thought it was funny!

Violet thought Virgil was mean for biting her tail! Violet didn't want to play anymore! Violet thought the tail in the face was funny. Violet was going to hit Virgil in the face with her tail, too! Violet was hitting Virgil in the face with her tail!

Thwack! Thwack! Thwack! Thwack! The telepathic equivalent of mischievous giggles rose up as the infants went back to being amused with each other.

Rose sighed and checked her wristwatch. She'd promised Henry they'd stay out of the apartment for at least two hours after he got home from class, which would hopefully give him enough time to study for the huge test he had next week. This had meant taking Virgil with her to her own classes, which had proven to be a disaster.

My notes from today's lectures were abominable, Rose thought in deep frustration. *I scarcely managed to take in half of what the professors said. And I have two of my own tests the day after Henry's. I understand that his grades represent our possible future income, while mine do not, but . . .*

Rose had always prided herself on her extraordinary grades. And more than that, she knew that having the best possible grades would be necessary for her to continue into graduate school to acquire the credentials she would need to go into paleontology.

But Henry's academic success was, unfortunately, even more important than that. If he failed any of his classes, it would take him longer to graduate, and the worse his grades were, the less likely it would become that he would find his way into a job that paid well. He had already failed two of his classes last semester, in fact, and was now retaking both of them.

This was a detail that Rose had only just learned last night. Henry had not felt the need to tell her about his two failed classes when he'd gotten the news. She'd had quite a struggle to control her temper when he'd finally informed her of that rather crucial detail last night.

After all, for crying out loud! Rose thought, her indignation rising again. *I was able to keep up my grades during our first few months of caring for Virgil! This despite the fact that I have a much longer walk to school, Henry insists that I do all the cooking, and we take equal turns with Virgil!*

Virgil was going to play leg face! Leg face would be fun!

Rose barely spared a glance at the roughhousing in the cage beside her. *Would it have killed him to at least inform me that he was struggling academically? I thought we had fixed this problem of him keeping secrets from me after he gave me control over the budget!*

Henry was, she had learned recently, appalling in his mathematical skill. She'd learned a few weeks ago that all the time she'd thought he was spending on the budget, he had actually been spending drawing.

Which was fine as far as it went. The incomprehensible mess of their finance book had been resolved when she had offered to take control of the budget, a duty he had been more than glad to relinquish.

But it turned out that her husband's ghastly skill at sums was extending to two of his college classes, as well. According to Henry, he needed both of those classes to graduate with his degree in biology, which made them nonnegotiable nightmares for him to navigate. He had, apparently, decided it would be wise to take both of those classes at once to get them over with.

And then Virgil had come into their lives early in the last semester, throwing their lives askew and disrupting everything.

It wasn't that Rose resented their son's awakening . . . but the timing had hardly been ideal. Couldn't the boy have waited until after Henry had finished his college education, at least?

But then again, if Virgil had taken longer, Henry might have found somebody else he wanted to marry, and perhaps wound up with a human infant to disrupt his schoolwork. It was only due to Virgil's timing that she and Henry had even met.

Rose sighed. Life, it seemed, was hardly ever convenient. Even when one thought they had their life all planned out, there were always new wrinkles standing in one's way.

Ow ow OWWWW! Violet didn't like claw face!

Rose jerked out of her thoughts and saw the wicked hooked claw of her son's back leg slashing at Violet's cheek. One of the blue scales on her cheek looked loose, and there was a line of blood welling up from it.

"VIRGIL!" she shouted, whamming the palm of her hand against the bars of the cage. "Stop that RIGHT NOW!"

Violet was sad! Violet was hurting! Violet was going to cry!

An unearthly, full-volume howl rose up from the cage. Virgil jerked back, releasing shock and startlement, and then he started screaming, as well.

Rose balled her fists up and clenched them over her eyes. It was all she could do to keep from screaming herself.

But she managed to control her temper, and focusing on soothing thoughts directed at the baby dragons caused them both to calm down again.

Virgil rolled across the floor of the cage, whapping his tail back and forth. He looked up at his mother.

That was a fun game. Virgil wanted to play claw face again.

Rose stared at him in exasperation.

We're going home now, she decided. *Henry can study at the library instead.*

CHAPTER 2
She

On the way back from apologizing to an irate zookeeper over the state of Violet's cheek, Rose pushed the pram back to the cage to allow her son the chance to say goodbye to his friend before they went home.

This proved to be a mistake.

Virgil wanted to go back in the cage! Virgil wanted to go back in the cage to play!

"Say goodbye," Rose said sternly. "That's what you're here for. You did not behave, so we're going home early."

Virgil was very sad! Virgil wanted to cry!

"Don't cry," Rose said sharply. "If you cry, we're going to leave right now."

Virgil was sad. Virgil was sulking. Virgil wanted to stay. Virgil wanted to go in the cage. Virgil wanted to play!

Another zookeeper was already in Violet's cage, treating her wound. As he finished, he cut a strip of Band-Aid of the right size and affixed it to her loose scale to hold it in place.

Rose watched with fascination. That brand of bandage had only just come out last year, and she'd never seen one in use before. The flesh-colored sticky disposable bandage looked silly on top of Violet's bright blue scales, but she could imagine how useful it might be with human children.

Virgil wriggled around in his pram and popped his head up through the blankets. Virgil had said hello to Violet. Could Virgil play with her now?

Rose ignored the audacious request, having no interest in the brazen ploy to get his own way despite what she had just told him. "Say goodbye, Virgil. Then we'll go home."

Virgil didn't want to go home! Virgil wanted to play with Violet! Virgil wanted to plaaaaaaaaaay!

"Your bucket is at home," Rose reminded him.

Oh. Virgil wanted to play with his bucket. Virgil wanted to play with his bucket now! Virgil wanted to go home!

"Say goodbye," Rose reminded him. "It's polite."

Virgil was saying goodbye to Violet! Virgil hoped to play claw face again soon!

"No!" the zookeeper and Rose said simultaneously.

The little blue dragon seemed uninterested in the farewell. She was busy trying to pry the strip of Band-Aid off with her front claw.

There was something funny on Violet's face. Why was there something funny on Violet's face? Violet didn't like this thing on her face. Violet wanted to get it off! Off! Off!

"Keep it on," the zookeeper said, swatting her claws away and holding his hand over the Band-Aid. "Your scale is loose. If we don't hold it on, it'll hurt you a lot."

Violet held still from her wriggling. She would be good. She wouldn't pull it off. She didn't want to hurt.

"Good," the zookeeper said, releasing her.

What was this sticky thing on Violet's face? Violet wanted it off! Off! Off!

Rose snorted with laughter as she turned the pram away from the cage. It seemed Virgil wasn't the only infant who behaved so terribly irrationally.

The flow of crowds was such that they always ebbed when one stopped at an exhibit and swelled when one most wanted to navigate through them, and such was the case as Rose sighed and waited for a stream of loud human children to walk past.

Virgil poked his head out of the pram to watch the parade of unfamiliar minds, and two of the human children stopped to poke their fingers at Virgil.

"Stop that!" Rose said sharply.

Both of the children persisted, and Virgil playfully batted at one of them with his back leg with the hooked claw.

"*No!*" Rose snapped, diving forward to seize the leg. All she needed was for someone's human child to be injured by her son today. Goodness knew what might result from that. The last thing her son's species needed was for humans to decide they were dangerous and force all *Deinonychus antirrhopus* infants to stay locked in cages.

Her temper in a rather frayed state, Rose scolded the two human children soundly, and they ran off to their mother crying about the mean lady. Their mother looked unsympathetic and gave them both a scolding about poking other people's pets.

Rose tried very hard not to let the word "pet" bother her. But nevertheless, it was all she could do to restrain the metaphorical steam rising from her ears as she waited for that bothersome family to continue on their way.

I did, at least, refrain from correcting her, she told herself. The last time she had corrected a wrongheaded woman at the zoo, it had resulted in the woman deciding to adopt a dragon of her own. Rose was still trying to convince herself that Bessie being a mother to a baby dragon wasn't a large catastrophe.

It wasn't exactly that she was concerned that Bessie and her husband Frank would not treat their son as intelligent. They seemed to be eager to do that much, at least. And after hearing Bessie grandly lecture Director Campbell about dragon's rights and the need for them, Rose had come to believe that the woman would be an asset to her son's species. But the two times Rose had run into the woman since then had been so *irritating.*

They had no human children. Philomel was still unhatched. And yet, Bessie had felt the need to give Rose very supercilious advice about taking care of Virgil.

With that *tone*.

That condescending, overbearing, patronizing, haughty, and imperious *tone*.

Mere months ago, Rose had wanted desperately to not be the only mother to a baby dragon in New York City. Now, she wanted there to be another mother to a baby dragon whom she could stand to be around.

Virgil peeked his head out of the pram, looking up at her with large and innocent eyes. It would have been adorable if his sharp teeth hadn't glinted from within his open mouth.

He wondered why his mother didn't just talk to that other baby's parents.

"Violet only has a father, Virgil," Rose told her son patiently. "Mr. Jones isn't married. Unless he is planning to change that in the near future, Violet has no mother."

No, not Violet's parents! That other baby's parents!

"I'm not fond of Philomel's parents."

No, not Crimson's parents! That *other* baby's parents!

"You mean the egg in the cage next to Violet?" Rose asked. "That egg doesn't have parents, Virgil. She hasn't even woken up all the way."

Virgil was confused. Why was Virgil's mother saying that? That baby had parents. They came to see her every day.

Rose sucked in her breath. "What?"

Virgil knew because Violet knew because Violet was there whenever they came. Violet knew, right?

Virgil's tail lashed confidently as he scrambled up on top of the pram and looked at Violet.

Violet wriggled out of the zookeeper's grip, rolled across the floor of the cage, and tried to claw at the Band-Aid on her cheek.

Uh huh. Violet knew that baby's parents. They had walked by Violet's cage after meeting their daughter, so she'd seen their memories of meeting the egg then. They were really quiet people. Violet had thought everyone knew about them. They came every day.

Rose's head jerked up to look at the zookeeper.

"That's . . . news to me, too," he said slowly. "When did this happen?"

Violet didn't remember. Oh, Violet remembered. Virgil was remembering for her. Virgil's mother had been mad at Crimson's mother while Violet had told Virgil about it happening.

Rose swallowed. *Weeks ago. That means it was weeks ago. Or one week, at the very least. The last time I saw Bessie was eight days ago.*

"Who in the world?" the zookeeper muttered.

Rose shared the man's sentiment. It was baffling.

Who were the fourth baby's parents, and why hadn't they said anything?

ℭHAPTER 3
Schoolwork

Forty minutes later, Rose burst through the door with Virgil under one arm and the handle of the pram she had dragged upstairs hooked around her other.

"Rose!" Henry protested, glancing at his wristwatch and looking up from a notebook he had been writing in. "You weren't supposed to be back for another hour!"

It was hardly a delightful welcome, but Rose wrestled the pram through the door and released Virgil without complaining at the words. Henry was, after all, justified in being cranky at his study time being interrupted.

"This is an emergency," she told him. "The fourth dragon egg has parents!"

Henry stared at her blankly.

Virgil was going to play in his bucket! Virgil was running to play in his bucket! Virgil was scrambling into his bucket! Virgil was going to hit a wall with his bucket!

Roll roll roll WHAM!

"Oh, and no one knows who they are yet," Rose went on, realizing she had to elaborate. "It's a mystery."

Henry kept staring at her.

"We have to figure out who they are!" Rose added, feeling that this explanation ought to be unnecessary.

Henry stirred at last and frowned. "Rose . . . I really couldn't care less about that right now. I'm trying to study to pass a test I don't want to take in the first place, and I'm not even half done. Could you please just . . . take Virgil out for a few more hours?"

Rose gaped at him. A few more *hours?* She had given him nine hours already, and had not been able to do anything with her own schoolwork during that period! What had he done with his time? Had he been drawing?

He had better not have spent the whole day drawing.

"Henry," she said, attempting to stay as calm as possible, "I apologize that I came home early. Clearly I was wrong that you'd be interested in the news *I* found incredibly riveting."

It seemed she hadn't managed to keep the irritation entirely out of her voice. She tried again.

"I can take Virgil back outside for another hour if you need it," she went on, trying to return to calm rationality. "Perhaps we can go shopping for the groceries for tomorrow night's dinner. But after that, I *need* to come home. I need you to take a turn watching Virgil. I have not been able to do any of my own schoolwork today, and I have a test upcoming, as well."

"Yes, but you always get good grades," Henry said tightly.

"That would be *because* I study, not because studying is optional for me!"

"Fantastic! I'm so glad to know that you getting an A instead of a B is more important than me passing a class instead of failing it!" Henry snarled, slamming his textbook shut.

"Of course it's important that you pass your test! That's why I've made a huge sacrifice of time for you today! I'm just saying that I need a turn! I need to study myself, Henry!"

WHAM! Virgil's bucket rolled into a wall again.

"Stop making all that noise!" Henry shouted, flinging his textbook onto the floor. It landed with a *thump.* Rose realized, to her horror, that Henry's frantic eyes were starting to look glassy.

"I'm sorry," Rose said hastily, running to pick up Virgil. "I'm sorry. I'll take him and be back in an hour. I'm sorry. I shouldn't have come back early. I'm sorry."

"Do whatever you want!" Henry cried. His eyes were wild and starting to leak. "It's not going to do any good, anyway! I'm going to fail it!"

Rose cast her mind around for some solution that might ameliorate his frenzy. "Can — can I go over things with you? Would it help if we review things together? I'm good at math. If we go over everything you're confused about one at a time —"

Henry took a deep breath. His eyes started to look less wild.

Virgil wriggled and squirmed to get out of Rose's arms. He was bored! He wanted his bucket! Why wouldn't his mother let him play in his bucket? It was unfair! He was going to scream! He was going to screaaaaaaaaaaaaaam!

Rose tried to shut Virgil's mouth, but she wasn't fast enough. A deafening screech burst forth from the tribulation in her arms.

Someone pounded on the ceiling from above them.

"*That!*" Henry shouted. "*That's* why I'm going to fail it! I can't possibly concentrate on anything with *him* around!"

Virgil's father didn't want him! Virgil's father was mad at him! Virgil was going to cryyyyyyyyyyyyyyy!

The deafening screams grew even louder.

In desperation, Rose dropped the tiny dragon on the couch and plugged her hands over her ears. Then a thought occurred to her, and she ran for the phone.

"What are you doing?" Henry shouted over the screams.

"Getting help!" Rose yelled back.

"Help from whom?"

There was someone on the other end of the party line. "Can you please hang up?" Rose broke into that conversation. "It's an emergency. I'll only take a few minutes. Then you can talk again. Please."

"Oh, all right, then," one of the voices on the line said.

"Talk to you in a minute, Eunice," the other voice said.

Thankfully, both women hung up.

"Help from *whom?*" Henry demanded.

But Rose was too busy asking the operator to connect her to her family's home.

"Mama?" she said as soon as the phone was answered. "Can I ask a favor? Henry and I both need to study, and we can't with Virgil around. Can you please watch him for a few hours?"

"We don't need help from your parents!" Henry shouted, his face turning red.

"One minute, Mama," Rose said. She put her hand over the phone. "Yes, we do, and you know it. There's no shame in that. Grammery lived with us for several years when I was a child, and she minded us all the time."

"I don't want to owe your father anything," Henry muttered. "He hates me."

"He's not the one I'm asking the favor from. And he doesn't. He just enjoys pestering people. You need to be a little less thin-skinned about it."

Henry didn't seem mollified.

Virgil's screaming stopped, and he helpfully projected a few memories of the last times they had visited Rose's family. Virgil's grandfather had called Virgil's father "the other one." Virgil's grandfather always said that. Virgil's grandfather thought it was very funny, so Virgil thought it was funny, too!

"It's not," Henry muttered.

Virgil thought it was very funny!

"It's not!"

"Mmm, I suppose we can take him for a few hours," Rose's mother said from the phone. "Will you be bringing him by, or would you like us to come pick him up?"

"Pick him up, please," Rose said in relief, removing her hand from the receiver. "Walking there and back would take up so much time as to defeat the purpose."

"All right. I'll have your father to get the car ready. We'll be over as soon as we can."

Rose hung up the phone and closed her eyes. She took a deep breath. *One crisis averted. Now to deal with another: Henry's ability to pass that test.*

Other one! Virgil thought it was very funny! Other one! Other one! He was going to keep shredding the couch.

"You're *what?*" Henry shouted, snatching the child up from the cushion. Sure enough, there were puncture wounds in the cushion under where his wicked back claws had been.

Virgil's tummy hurt now. He was going to —

Henry yelped and spun the baby around. Virgil let out a fiery belch that scorched the wall beside them.

Now Virgil's diaper felt uncomfortable. It was wet. It was wet, wet, wet, wet, wet! He wanted it off! He was going to shred it with his back feet!

Rose barely dove in time to stop him. The last thing they needed was to have to buy more cloth diapers. The child had already destroyed too many of them, and melted or chewed on an appalling number of safety pins.

"How long until your parents get here?" Henry demanded.

CHAPTER 4
Studying

Quiet reigned without their son present, and it seemed very strange.

"Have we ever had this time alone together before?" Henry murmured, looking up from his textbook.

Rose looked up from her notebook, as well. "I don't know," she said slowly. "I don't think so. Perhaps while Virgil was napping."

"Doesn't count," Henry said, shaking his head.

"Well, then, almost certainly no."

Henry set down his book. "Do you realize that we never actually took time for a proper courtship?"

". . . Yes," Rose said. "We were a little rushed. But don't you need to study?"

"This is more important."

Oh, for goodness's sake, no it isn't!

Henry brightened, setting his textbook down. "We should do something nice for Valentine's Day!"

"Mmm," Rose said noncommittally. She had no interest in the silly holiday, but she supposed they could do something if he cared about it. "But right now, you need to study."

"I'm going to fail anyway." He sounded downright cheerful about it. "We might as well spend this time together."

Rose stared at him in exasperation. "You're not going to fail. I taught you all those formulae, didn't I?"

"Out of my head already." He waved a finger near his temple and made a whooshing noise.

"Then you can study harder," she said acerbically.

"Or I can accept the inevitable and stop worrying about it." He grinned. "C'mere and give me a kiss."

"I shall do so," Rose informed him, "when you have earned it by reciting one of the formulae that you claim has whooshed out of your mind."

He groaned. "Slave driver."

"I want you to pass," Rose said. "You have married a woman who cares about grades. You have informed me that yours matter, as well. Thus, I shall make sure you do well at yours."

"But I hate it!" Henry whined.

"Just get past these two classes," Rose assured him. "Then you'll be back to your true love: biology."

"I hate my major," Henry groaned. "I wanted to go to an art school, but my family insisted I go to college instead."

Rose jerked a little to the side. Well, that was . . . surprising and unsettling news.

"Did you not want to be able to support a family?" she asked before she could stop herself.

Henry pouted. He seemed to be in a childish mood. "You sound like my father. 'Nobody makes any money at art!'"

Rose hesitated. Mindful of not starting another fight when they had just barely escaped the last one, she said cautiously, "I'm sure there are some who do."

"But not many. I know, I know, I know," Henry groaned, shaking his head. "That's why I let my father talk me into it. But I wish he hadn't. You'd have still married me if I'd been in art school, right?"

Um, Rose thought. That was a difficult question to answer, seeing as she hadn't experienced it. It was possible, but she doubted she would have been thrilled about it. She had grown to love Henry now, but they had been strangers initially.

"I suspect my father would have been less eager to give his permission if he'd known that you intended to pursue art as a career," she said diplomatically.

Henry's face clouded over. "It's not fair, is it? The way I'm expected to do something I hate instead of what I'm good at."

Rose opened her mouth to remind him that, being a man and a father, he had a duty to provide for his family, and he should know that. But then it occurred to her that there were many people who would raise similar objections to a woman and a mother who wished to go into a complex science field.

She sighed. "Perhaps it would have been better if we'd never met one another, or Virgil. Both of us would have found it easier to pursue our chosen occupations had we been single."

Henry's head jerked back. "Don't say that! Never say that! You two are the best things that have ever happened to me!"

Rose gave him a doubtful stare. "That's absolutely not true. Our son is such a bother, and I am . . . hardly a typical wife. You must find us difficult to live with."

"Not true," Henry said obstinately.

"Is it not?" Rose asked, pointing to her textbook. "The fact that I will not give up my goals makes your life more difficult."

Henry paused. He hesitated. "All right, there may be some truth to that. But it's this blasted schoolwork that's the problem. Not you. Or Virgil. I love you."

"Me, or Virgil?"

"Both, obviously, although the boy not quite so much when he's screaming."

Rose smiled slightly.

"But really, you aren't the problem," Henry insisted. "I wanted to be married and to have kids. I chose this. I'm glad I have it. What I *didn't* choose was the blasted math classes."

"That doesn't mean you wouldn't have been happier with a more normal family," Rose said in a low voice.

She should, perhaps, have left the subject alone, but she couldn't leave the point unsaid. It had been weighing on her for a long time.

Chapter 4: Studying

"Pshaw!" Henry waved that aside. "Being the first couple to raise a baby dragon is a pain in the neck, but sometimes it's so exciting, I want to burst with pride. Virgil's a blessing more than a curse."

Rose blinked back tears, determined not to let Henry see. The times when she felt like a failure as a mother were exceeded only by the times when she felt like a failure as a wife. She simply was not romantic by nature, and her husband was.

Left to herself, she didn't think she would have ever married. She hadn't ever been fully opposed to the idea, but the thought of husband or children had never been a high priority in her mind. She simply didn't think she would have bothered.

And yet, here she was, with both husband and child while still not having achieved her dream. She could not give it up, would not, although she knew that would continue to make life more difficult for her husband and child.

Sometimes she even questioned why she cared so much about paleontology, given that she had a real-life dragon living with her. But a living dragon was not the same as a fossil. A living dragon was a person who had to be loved and cared for. A fossil was a mystery to be solved.

The mysteries to solve riveted her and took her breath away. The duty of caring for an infant was exhausting, not enlightening. And as long as she held to her promise to herself that she would never treat him as a subject to study from a cold and analytical perspective, it would always be that way.

While she loved Henry and Virgil, she also knew that her emotion was far more reserved than Henry's, and certainly more reserved than the wildly uninhibited infant's.

Knowing that made her feel inadequate. It made her feel like she was not enough, and never could be. Sometimes she thought, *If only . . .*

If only she had not met Henry.

If only she had not met Virgil.

If only her life had stayed on the simple, single track that she had planned to stay on for her entire life.

Why had she veered off into this tangent?

Why had she ended up in this position where her only option was to fail, and fail, and fail all over again?

"Is something wrong?" Henry asked.

Rose shook her head, turning her face away.

"Well, you know if you don't tell me, I can just ask Virgil what it is," Henry joked.

Rose gave him a livid glare.

"Or not," he said quickly. "Or not. But, um . . . can you please tell me? Did I do something wrong?"

Rose looked down at the carpet for a long moment.

"I am not a wife who darns your socks," she said finally. "You want a wife who darns your socks."

"Is that what this is about?" Henry asked incredulously. "The *socks?*"

"No!" Rose said angrily. "It's about you not thinking my tests matter as much as yours do! It's about the fact that I think you should've married somebody who's happy to be your housemaid, because I'm not that, and I'm never going to be, and I don't *want* to be! If that's my role, what am I? I'm a *failure!*"

"I'll do it myself!" Henry said defensively. "I said I would! I can mend my own socks! I just hate doing it!"

"You keep putting them back on the couch every morning that it's my turn to watch Virgil, as if you're hoping that I'll do them for you if you just leave them there long enough."

Henry bit his lip, looking guilty. "Well . . ."

Rose picked up her textbook. "I need to study."

"And apparently I need to mend my socks," Henry muttered, getting up from the couch. "Beats studying, anyway."

He started to walk off towards the bedroom.

Rose lowered her textbook a fraction of an inch. "Wait. Come here."

"Why?" he asked, looking baffled.

She smiled slightly. "Because that deserves a kiss."

CHAPTER 5
Solved

Rose felt less than confident about Henry's chances of passing his test the next day, seeing as he had spent the entire rest of the evening mending his socks instead of studying, but she could hardly complain, seeing as he had been doing it for her sake.

Despite her trying to dissuade him from spending the entire evening on that activity, he had stubbornly persisted, and then insisted on taking Virgil out of the house for a walk after his grandparents brought him back, so that Rose could have time studying.

Which she appreciated, but she . . . *did* want him to pass his tests, too.

Before he left, Henry jokingly held out one of his textbooks to Virgil. "Want to breathe fire on this?"

The sleepy dragon opened one eye.

Virgil wasn't burpy right now. Virgil didn't want to chew things, either. Maybe he could claw it instead.

He sleepily reached out a claw at the book.

"Henry!" Rose cried. "Don't give him ideas!"

Henry snickered and tossed the book overhead, then dropped it on the couch.

"Your mother's right, Virgil," he said with mock solemnity. "Only destroy my textbook *after* I've passed the class and don't need it anymore."

Okay. Virgil would remember. He would wait until his father said to breathe fire on it.

"Don't do it at all!" Rose cried.

Henry left the house whistling, seeming entirely carefree.

Rose watched him go with mixed feelings.

While her husband seemed much more cheerful now, and that was certainly a good thing, she hoped he hadn't given up on passing those tests completely.

After eating her breakfast and scrubbing the dishes clean, Virgil came crawling into the kitchen.

He was hungry. Could Virgil eat breakfast? He wasn't sure if he should burn that book yet.

"Breakfast yes, breathing fire on books no," Rose said sternly. "Your father was just joking. You should never do that."

Virgil didn't understand, but Virgil was hungry and wanted food now. Could Virgil have his breakfast?

"Say please," Rose instructed. She was trying to teach their son manners.

Could Virgil have his please?

"Close enough."

She served him breakfast, and as she was doing so, she found her mind wandering to the mystery she'd learned about yesterday. If the fourth dragon had parents, why hadn't they come forward? What reason could they have for keeping silent?

She badly wanted to meet them and ask, but it wasn't like she could predict when they would be in front of the cage.

Oh, Virgil knew when they would be there. They always came in the morning. Violet said so.

The small dragon's head ducked down as he munched out of the bowl she'd left on the floor for him.

Rose paused. "How early in the morning?"

They always came after Violet's breakfast. Virgil liked breakfast. Virgil was eating his breakfast now. It was yummy.

Rose's mind worked feverishly. Violet usually had breakfast at nine o'clock. Right now, it was eight twenty. If they started getting ready immediately and walked quickly . . .

Virgil's head poked up from the bowl. Were they going to see Violet? Virgil wanted to see Violet! Virgil wanted to go right now!

That decided it, of course.

"Yes, we're going to see Violet," Rose said.

Preparing the pram for their perambulation, Rose reflected that perhaps her son was spending too much time at the zoo for her liking. It was only natural because the child could not be trusted around human infants, and Violet was the only other dragon egg who had hatched, and thus she was his only playmate. But if another dragon egg hatched . . .

Philomel was close to hatching. But taking Virgil to play with Bessie's son on a regular basis seemed a dreadful option. Rose had had enough of the woman's pompous attitude to last a lifetime.

But a fourth egg . . .

A fourth egg who would not live in the zoo, who would have parents that Rose could stand to be around . . .

That would solve so many problems.

The walk to Central Park Zoo seemed to go quickly, as it always did now that she'd traveled the route so many times, despite the fact that it went no faster than normal in terms of time spent: a little over twenty minutes.

There was a slight delay when Virgil sneezed and set his blanket alight, resulting in a horrified scream from a passerby, but Rose beat that out with rapid familiarity born of entirely too much practice, and then assured the panicked woman that her baby was, in fact, the source of the flames, and had not been a victim of a stray cigar dropped carelessly upon him.

Then she had to deal patiently with the woman's shock that the baby wasn't human.

Still, events such as those were extremely commonplace, more's the pity, so she arrived at the zoo with very little delay and no further thought about the incident.

Virgil was ecstatic to see his friend.

He poked his head out of the pram and swished his tail back and forth, which lashed the blanket along with it until it flopped to the ground. Rose scooped the blanket up, reflecting that since it was charred in a corner, it would require washing tonight anyway, so a little dirt would not harm the child.

Virgil was saying hello to Violet! Virgil was excited to see Violet! Virgil wanted to play tail face!

Violet was busy. Virgil should come back later.

Virgil's tail lashed harder, and he emanated indignation. That wasn't fair! He wanted to play!

What is Violet busy doing? Rose started to wonder, but the question was answered even before she finished the thought.

A memory of Violet's mother washed over her.

She was a beautiful, vain dragon, vibrantly blue, the most beautiful dragon in the whole wide world, except her daughter was even more beautiful. She stretched out her long neck to show off her horns to her prospective mate who she'd already married. Her purple husband ignored her, so she snorted sparks at him. Must he be clueless? She had been hoping to be coy. Their daughter was going to bonk him with her horns when he got home for being so silly.

Rose sighed aloud as the scene continued, and pulled herself out of the not-really-quite-a-memory.

She knew this memory well. It was one Violet loved to share with curious crowds. Rose had experienced it six times now, which is why she had no problem divorcing herself from the experience this time, unlike the rest of the crowd. But the memory had changed a great deal since Violet had first shared it.

It was now muddled with the future and from a childish perspective, and it kept including recollections of incidents that had never happened, such as Violet-as-a-hatchling interacting with her birth parents.

In other words, it was now far more a product of Violet's imagination than a true memory from her mother, and yet, she portrayed it as if it were true.

This is going to be a problem in the future, Rose reflected. *How many people are going to trust these "recollections" as fact when they are, in fact, sometimes closer to fiction?*

It was particularly disturbing when she reflected that the easily-muddled memories of these infants' ancestors would be the only clues their human parents would have as to what was normal for the children in each developmental stage. How much of the information they were likely to rely on would be accurate by the time these children came of age?

It was much like having an oral tradition rather than written records. And Rose knew of no way to record memories in a more trustworthy and dependable way.

As the more-or-less-daydream progressed, Virgil poked his tail out of the blanket and lashed it back and forth.

Virgil was bored. Violet was boring. Virgil wanted to go play with the other baby.

"She hasn't hatched yet, Virgil," Rose reminded him.

But Virgil wanted to go play with the other baby! She was awake! The other baby's parents were playing with her now!

What?! Rose's head whipped around to look at the people nearest the other cage. *They're here already?!*

CHAPTER 6
Surprise

At first, she thought, *It couldn't be them.* She looked for another couple standing near the cage with the egg. But everyone else in the crowd near them was walking elsewhere, watching Violet, or staring off into space.

If only two people were currently watching the unhatched egg, those had to be the people Virgil had referred to.

Rose sucked in her breath.

She should not have been shocked. It should, in fact, have been obvious that it would happen sooner or later. A fetus could not see what humans looked like, nor would a dragon care if they could. After all, the shape of humans was so alien compared to their own form that all humans probably looked alike to them.

The parents were colored.

It's not 1821, Rose thought frantically. *It's 1921. I can walk over there and make their acquaintance.*

She could, she knew she could, but her feet stayed frozen in place. She was terrified to take even a single step forward. This was outside any of her social experience. Was she *allowed* to talk to them? Was that even something that was *done?*

She tried to think of what her mother would say. But her imagination failed her.

How could she possibly know what was appropriate and what wasn't in this instance? In all her years of school, in her neighborhood, in all her family's social circles, it was simply a question that had never come up.

Cowardice rose in her throat, and she started to consider fleeing before Violet or Virgil announced her presence.

Why was Virgil's mother running away?

Rose froze. She looked down at her questioning son, who now seemed very confused.

She swallowed deeply. Did she want Virgil to grow up to believe that external appearance meant everything?

No. Because he wasn't just a different color. He was a different *shape*.

Perhaps . . . perhaps it didn't matter what the rules were. Perhaps it didn't matter if there *were* rules. There had been no rules laid out when she'd adopted Virgil, and she had done it anyway, because it had felt like the right thing to do.

She could transcend species. Surely she could do something much more trivial.

Choosing to accept Virgil was the most difficult thing she'd ever done. But putting one foot in front of the other right now was the second most difficult. She pushed through the crowd around Violet's cage, reaching the other side and the empty expanse in which only two people stood.

Both of them had their back to Rose, and now that she was much closer, she realized there was a silent conversation going on between them. Almost a one-way conversation, in fact.

The eggbound dragon was . . . chattering?

Her feathery, fleeting impressions were nothing like Virgil's insistent nagging, Philomel's demanding fury, or Violet's exuberant flamboyance. They came and went rapidly, so fast that Rose could barely take in the images, and the range was so short that Rose didn't even notice they were happening until she was nearly behind the two parents.

It was like the new dragon was whispering. Whispering at an insane speed.

The two parents turned around at once.

"Um," Rose said, gulping, "hello. I'm Rose Palmer. Wainscott, I mean. Rose Wainscott. I was only recently married, so I'm not used to it yet. Pleased to make your acquaintance."

The man and woman both stared at her. Their expressions were not unfriendly, but they were not particularly chummy, either. They both stared at her silently.

Panic fluttered in Rose's throat. Had she truly broken some rule of propriety? Were they judging her harshly for that? She didn't know. Why had she felt the need to go over to them? What had she thought could be gained?

"And . . . y-your names?" she asked nervously.

The silence stretched on, and Rose tried to distract herself by looking at their clothing. The man's tweed suit was shabby at the elbows, and the woman wore a shirtwaist and a long, pleated skirt. His hat was a fedora with black ribbon, while hers was a tight-fitting cloche that wasn't really in fashion.

Virgil poked his head out from behind the blanket, and his clawed forelegs followed as he pulled himself up on the side of the pram.

Hello! Virgil was saying hello! Virgil wanted to meet the other baby! Virgil thought she'd be more interesting than Violet, who was being boring. Hello! Virgil was saying hello to the other baby!

A smile split across the woman's face. "Oh! You're the one Ophelia keeps talking about." Her voice was quiet, much like the eggbound dragon's telepathic equivalent. "She says you've been wanting to meet us. It's a pleasure."

Rose breathed a desperate sigh of relief. "Yes. A pleasure," she said rapidly. "I didn't know, um . . ."

. . . *that you were* . . . No, no, she couldn't say that! That had to be taboo.

". . . that her name was Ophelia," she finished frantically.

The man smiled slightly. "We love Shakespeare," he said. His voice was quiet, too.

"How long has it been since she chose you?" Rose asked.

Husband and wife exchanged looks.

"It happened on the second day she was here," the man said in a low voice. "We've come to see her every day since."

Rose stared at him in astonishment. It was unfathomable.

"Why did you not talk to the zoo staff? You should ask to bring her home with you before she hatches!"

The two looked at each other.

The woman said quietly, "We didn't particularly want to be told no."

Rose felt a sudden, stabbing shame. Of course they had to worry about that. Why, she had been afraid to even walk over and start a conversation. What would happen if Director Campbell refused point-blank? What if he chose to have the newest dragon transferred into another zoo to get her away from them?

It wasn't implausible. She knew nothing about the man's character save that he had been extremely unenthusiastic about both Virgil and Philomel being raised outside of a zoo. It was easy to imagine that he would take any pretext to keep the next dragon child in a cage forever.

Still, something had to be done. Not speaking up wouldn't deliver that little girl to her parents' home.

Unless they didn't want her at home. Violet's father was content to have her stay here. An entirely different fear knotted in Rose's stomach. Suppose their idea of what was appropriate for *Deinonychus antirrhopus* was entirely different from hers?

To her surprise, the baby dragon answered that in rapid impressions, most of them too fast for Rose to catch. The only ones she was sure of were the ones that said that yes, she wanted to go home with her parents, and also it was empty and it wasn't supposed to be.

Rose was puzzled, trying to work that out.

"The cradle," the woman said softly. "Our other child died."

Her husband reached over and squeezed her hand softly.

Rose couldn't even fathom such a loss, and she didn't want to try. The thought of it made her feel split down the middle.

Better not to think about it. Better to do something useful. What could she do that would be useful right now?

Ah. Yes. Of course. She could introduce them to the man who would determine their family's fate.

"Would the two of you be willing to remain here while I bring Director Campbell?" Rose asked. "He runs the American Museum of Natural History, and is the one with legal ownership of the dragon eggs. He can give permission for you two to take Ophelia home."

The man seemed hesitant. He looked at his wife.

She shook her head. They seemed to be holding a silent conversation. There was neither voice nor telepathic impression, except from Virgil, who started to let out feelings of being bored and chewing on his blanket. Ooh, now he would shred it!

Rose rescued the blanket from him.

At last, the man said, "No. What we have now is enough. We don't want to jeopardize that."

A flickering impression of deep offense rose from the egg.

If her parents didn't want her, she would refuse to hatch. She would die. If her parents didn't want her, she would refuse to hatch. And she'd die.

The woman sucked in her breath, her shoulders tensing. She looked shocked, on the verge of tears.

"Ophelia," the man said sharply, his volume raising for the first time. "That is not right. Don't say that!"

If Ophelia's parents didn't want her, she would rather die. She was starving already. She should have hatched weeks ago. She refused to hatch if she had to stay here with the prying minds and the other baby who was always loud and talking. She'd told them she was hungry. She'd thought they knew what that meant. If she had to stay here, she wouldn't hatch. She would die.

The man's eyes darkened. He started to talk, and his voice failed him. He tried again, and he finally managed it, his voice shaking. "All right. Please bring the director here."

CHAPTER 7
Suitable

Hurrying back with a sour-faced director in tow, Rose stopped as far as possible from the dragon cages and pointed at the cage that contained the egg. "Those are her parents. They are really very suitable."

Director Campbell's pinched face said otherwise. "You didn't mention they were colored."

"I didn't mention that because it has no bearing," Rose said defensively, though she had expected that reaction, and it was why she had stopped so far from earshot to point out the child's parents. "For all we know, the dragon will have brown or black scales. In any case, she isn't human in the first place."

The man looked unimpressed with her impeccable logic. "Well, I suppose the dragon's life is of prime concern," he said begrudgingly. "I'll talk to them."

He started forward, elbowing his way through the crowd to reach the cage that contained the egg. Wrestling with the pram through the crowd around Violet's cage, Rose was left an increasing number of paces behind.

As they passed within range of Violet's telepathy, Rose found herself immersed in yet another highly-fictionalized vision of events, this one of Violet and her parents flying through the sky and hunting together over a New York City skyline.

Rose severely hoped that no one here was gullible enough to believe that was an unaltered memory.

Virgil noticed how near to Violet's cage they were walking. He climbed halfway up the side of the pram in excitement. Virgil wanted to play with Violet! Did Violet want to play with him now?

Violet, thoroughly engrossed in her daydream, barely even bothered to respond. There was a faint hint of rebuff, then a determined resurgence of her dream.

Virgil was very mad! Violet was being boring! Virgil didn't like Violet! Virgil would play with the other baby instead!

The daydream now demonstrated Violet breathing fire at an annoying, loud insect to catch it on fire.

Rose chuckled at the metaphor despite herself.

Virgil was really mad!

Rose bit her lip to hide her mirth as she pushed Virgil back down into the pram and replaced the blanket. She had no wish for him to become a second source of curiosity to the audience gathered here.

But as before, Violet was really a remarkable distraction. It was a testament to how engrossed the audience was that nobody seemed to notice either Virgil's interruption or his appearance when he popped his head stubbornly out of the blanket again.

Rose might have found this lack of awareness disturbing if she had not witnessed the same phenomenon many times before. When one was not used to speaking with dragons, it could be difficult to spare any concentration for the world around oneself. She'd experienced it herself, so while it might be rather unsettling to witness, as a source of concern, it was minimal.

Unless, of course, one's path became obstructed by a man who would not move aside to let one's pram through, even when one asked said man politely, and then several more times with increasing temper, to please do so.

Director Campbell had already reached the other cage and was now speaking with Ophelia's parents. It was maddening that she could not hear a word.

Rose finally resorted to pushing the man physically aside. He stumbled forward, blinked, looked at her reproachfully, and then turned back to stare forward at Violet's cage.

Rose fumed as she stormed forward with the pram.

Virgil was happy! Virgil was excited! The other baby was going to hatch, and he was going to play tail-face with her!

"That's not going to happen today, Virgil," Rose muttered under her breath. "Your hatching took several hours, and Violet's took most of a day. Besides, you were not permitted to play with her until she was over a week old, in case of fragility."

Virgil wanted to play tail-face! Virgil wanted to play tail-face!

They reached the edge of the crowd and neared the three adults conversing. Disappointingly, it seemed the conversation had been short and Rose had missed most of it.

". . . provisionally," Director Campbell was saying. "But I'll send someone over twice a day to check on her health, and if there's any sign of malnutrition, she'll be coming back here for good. The dragon's health is of prime importance."

"Yes, we agree." The quiet man looked profoundly relieved. He nodded rapidly. "We only want what's best for her."

"Hmmm." Director Campbell gave both of the parents a suspicious eye flicker. "Yes, so do I. Very well. Come with me. We'll make the arrangements. Good day, Mrs. Wainscott."

He barely nodded his head in Rose's direction before he stalked off. Ophelia's parents followed him, though the woman stopped to give a slight wave and mouth, "Thank you."

Rose took a deep breath and stared at the silent egg.

"I'm glad you have your parents now," she said.

Ophelia didn't respond.

"I'd like to think I helped a little," Rose added.

The egg didn't respond.

Rose's eyebrows drew together. It was most infuriating. First she had been cut out of the entire conversation, and now even the egg was ignoring her. All right, this was perhaps not her personal concern, but she had a right to want to know what was going on with a new dragon egg, didn't she?

Never mind what Henry's answer to that question would be.

Virgil's mother was just like Virgil's aunts! He had spent time with them yesterday! Virgil's mother was nosy!

"I am not nosy!" Rose exclaimed.

An impression of her younger sisters' mischievous giggles bubbled up from her son's pram.

Nosy! Nosy! Virgil's mother was nosy! Virgil thought it was very funny!

"Interested is not the same as inquisitive!" Rose insisted.

Nosy! Nosy! They had broken into Virgil's grandfather's study yesterday. He had been very upset to find them going through all his things. He had called them nosy. Virgil thought that was very funny. Nosy! Nosy!

It would seem, Rose thought with disgruntlement, *that there are disadvantages to asking one's family to watch one's child for a day.*

For a change of pace, and because she had no eagerness to return home to face the household chores she knew awaited her, Rose chose to take the slightly longer route of 5th Avenue, rather than her usual path through Central Park.

This proved to be a mistake.

"Oh, Rose!" a familiar voice called from behind her.

Rose's shoulders tensed. She knew that voice all too well. She turned around slowly to face her dreaded compatriot.

"Hello, Mrs. Bailey," she said stiffly.

"Oh, never mind that, call me Bessie," the woman said grandly, adjusting her hat. It was adorned with a peacock feather twice as tall as her head. "It's a lovely day for a walk, isn't it? Philomel and I are out enjoying it."

Rose glanced behind the woman, and sure enough, there was the nanny, thirty paces behind her, pushing a shiny pram that contained a large, dusky orange egg with brown spots. The egg was much too far away to be within telepathic range.

Chapter 7: Suitable

"I see you and your son are spending quality time together," Rose said sarcastically.

"Yes, it's glorious, isn't it?" Bessie beamed. "I thought he'd benefit from a small change of scene."

He hasn't hatched yet! Rose wanted to scream. *He can't see the scene!*

This prompted her son to poke his head up through the blankets and make commentary.

Virgil could see the scene! Virgil liked seeing the scene. Virgil was clawing the blanket! Virgil liked clawing the blanket. Virgil's claw was caught in the blanket. Virgil's claw was caught in the blankeeeeeeeeeeet!

Rose wrenched the enormous curved back claw out of the hole in the cloth he had burned earlier today.

"Did I tell you what I learned about dragons yesterday?" Bessie asked in her most officious tone.

Please don't. Rose smiled brittlely.

"I learned that dragons are warm-blooded. It means their blood is hot instead of cold. That's why they breathe fire. Did you know that?"

Rose stared at the woman, flabbergasted. *That's not what it means! It has to do with how their circulatory systems are arranged!*

"I see you didn't," Bessie said smugly. She glanced down at Virgil, and then wrinkled her nose. "Ugh! Don't you ever have that blanket washed? It's filthy! One would think you don't care about his health at all —"

"It was very nice to see you, but I simply must be going now!" Rose said rapidly, bursting forward and taking off at a run.

There was only so much of Bessie she could cope with in one day.

CHAPTER 8
Shrill

Before the week was out, Henry had the results of the two tests he had studied so hard for.

It was not the best news Rose had ever heard.

"I passed *one* of them!" he said triumphantly, his face bright, as he entered the apartment. "That means I have a chance of passing that class this time! Since the other one's a lost cause, I'll just stop going to that one and take it again next semester."

Rose tried very, very hard to suppress a long sigh. "Shall we set aside a time every week for you to study for the one you're going to attempt to finish?"

"No, I'll just do it when I need to," he said.

"Regular studying would probably help," she hinted.

"I'd rather not," he shot back. "Besides, I have three other classes this semester that I need to do well in. I might pass the math one or I might not. How are yours?"

Rose was silent. She supposed he would only be irritated if she complained about the A minus she had received for her most recent test, even though she had been greatly displeased about it. "I am going to need to study more carefully."

"So, no change, then," Henry said, rubbing his shoulders. "How is Virgil?"

Virgil had behaved! Could he come out of the box now?

"What's this?" Henry asked, glancing down the hallway. "What box does he mean?"

"The new time-out box," Rose said sharply.

Virgil didn't like this box! The box was very boring! Could he come out of the box now?

Henry headed down the hallway to the bathroom and opened the door. Rose followed him. Virgil was inside a wooden crate that was inside the bathtub. Wet towels were draped over everything flammable, including the back of the door.

"You realize that the crate is flammable, right?" Henry asked.

"I realize that if he burns it down, I'll buy another one."

"Awwwwww, poor thing," Henry crooned, leaning down and scooping up the dragon. "Is Mommy being mean? Of course you can come out. You're not going to set anything on fire now, are you?"

"He had better not," Rose said darkly. "He burned the pram this morning."

Henry paused. "He did what?"

"He burned the pram," Rose repeated. "And he did it on purpose, too. He was commenting on how much fun it would be to have it on fire before he breathed fire on it. I am very upset with him right now."

Virgil's father shouldn't listen to Virgil's mother! Virgil wanted to stay out of the box! Virgil's mother was being mean!

Henry swore under his breath.

Rose agreed with the sentiment, though she wouldn't use such language herself. "So I asked our neighbors if they had a box we could keep, and they gave me that one. I told him he could stay there for a good long while."

Alarm radiated off their son as he wriggled in Henry's arms to get his attention.

Virgil had behaved and he hadn't sneezed on purpose and it wasn't his fault that he'd accidentally set the pram on fire and also he'd behaved. He didn't want to be in the box anymore and he had behaved and his mother was being mean and he was going to behave!

"What are we going to do?" Henry groaned, setting the objecting dragon back in the crate. "We need a pram."

"I know," Rose said grimly. "We can't take him anywhere without a conveyance to put him in. Quite apart from people staring, he is getting increasingly heavy."

Could Virgil play in his bucket now?

"NO!" both of his parents shouted.

Virgil was very sad! He was going to cry!

"If you scream, we'll shut the door," Rose told him.

Virgil was going to cry even louderrrrrrrr!

In less than a minute, he was alone in the bathroom with the door closed.

"So," Henry said, raising his voice to be heard over the shrill howls, "what do we do next? I suppose we could have him crawl everywhere."

"Would you let a six-month-old human crawl all over the sidewalks of New York?" Rose queried.

Henry frowned. "No, I wouldn't. Health concerns aside . . ."

"Health concerns aside . . ." Rose agreed.

All sorts of disasters might happen if Virgil were allowed to roam free. He might scamper off and get lost. He might be kidnapped by some unscrupulous person. He might run into the road and collide with a car or a horse. He might sneeze upon a nearby leg, causing panic and injury. Essentially, there were all kinds of safety hazards that would be associated with his locomotion being under his own power out in public, and none of those could be addressed until the boy was old enough to have something resembling common sense.

"There's such a thing as a leash," Henry suggested.

Rose cringed.

"I mean, it would be cheaper than a pram."

"And it would make him look like a pet, and it would not address half of the health and safety concerns, and given that he isn't even close to walking upright, I don't think he has the stamina to crawl for the same distances we walk every day."

Henry sighed. "I know, I know. So what do we do?"

"I've asked all of our acquaintances I could think of if they had a spare pram," Rose said.

"Did any of them?"

"No, but perhaps I have forgotten someone."

"Your parents?" Henry suggested.

"I asked them first. Mama gave away their baby things a long time ago."

"My parents?" Henry asked.

"I haven't called them yet, but you're welcome to. I did call your brother, who says they don't have an additional one."

Henry's brother had given them the original pram.

"If he doesn't have an extra one, my parents won't, either," Henry said. "I assume you asked the neighbors?"

"I did, and unsurprisingly, none of them did. I was lucky enough to have gotten hold of the crate."

"I suppose we could ask the Baileys . . ."

Rose didn't even try to hide her horror at the prospect.

"I mean, they certainly have money."

"They certainly do. And I'm certain we do not have a strong enough acquaintanceship to ask them to buy something for us," Rose said flatly. "Quite apart from the fact that I would not want to ask *anyone* to buy things for us, I have no desire to be in Mrs. Bailey's debt. I would sooner buy a brand new pram ourselves."

"Well, is that out of the question?" Henry asked.

Rose hesitated. The correct answer was, *Any unnecessary money spent is out of the question as long as you're going to keep failing classes and having to retake them.* But that was not something she could say.

"Hang on!" Henry said, snapping his fingers. "A wagon! My parents have an old one I used to use as a child."

"It would be wood," Rose objected.

"It would be free," Henry retorted.

"But if Virgil combusts it . . . how great would the nostalgic loss be? I wouldn't want him to destroy one of your favorite toys from childhood."

Henry shrugged. "I'd be very annoyed, but not heartbroken. I liked it, but I'm not nostalgically attached to it. Besides, think about how much smaller it would be. We could fit it in a closet rather than keeping it in a corner, so Virgil would be less able to reach it to sneeze on it in the first place."

It was a good solution. Rose opened her mouth to agree, but then the phone rang.

Henry ran to answer it. "Wainscott residence, Henry speaking."

As he listened to the voice on the other end of the line, Henry's face went pale.

"Just a minute," he said, and pulled the phone away from his ear. "Hey, Rose, can you spare me for the rest of the day, and perhaps tomorrow, as well?"

"Why?" Rose asked, startled.

"The new little girl dragon is hatching, and it looks like there may be trouble. Something to do with her waiting too long to hatch. They want as many people there as possible who can help, and since I have experience taking care of Virgil . . ."

Rose's heart squeezed. "Yes. Go."

CHAPTER 9
Specimens

Mr. Teedle came and picked up Henry ten minutes later. He barely spared a moment for a greeting before the two left.

Rose watched them go with a number of mixed feelings. First, she hoped desperately that the problem was not as severe as it sounded, and that Henry would be of some use. The only thing that mattered was that the child be born healthy.

But she had other, less charitable feelings, as well.

She was rather upset that Mr. Teedle had asked for Henry's help, and not hers.

Of course she understood that it would make no sense to ask both of them to come, because one of them had to remain behind with Virgil. Having another dragon underfoot at the new dragon's hatching would no doubt complicate matters rather than aiding them.

But still. What made Henry more qualified to help than her? Rose had spent as much time with their son as he had. She was also the one who was studying dragons, and the one who had taken more of an interest in Ophelia in the first place.

Not to mention that Mr. Teedle had known her far longer than Henry. In any matter involving dragons, he should have thought of her first.

Moodily, Rose prepared Virgil's usual dinner of chicken, water, and raw eggs, wishing as she always did that the boy would learn to eat a cheaper meat, such as pork.

She walked down the hall to the bathroom, where she found her son curled up in a ball with his tail tucked around him, snoring softly.

Rose smiled wryly. A few hours ago, she had wanted nothing more than for him to take a nap and leave her alone. Now that she wanted him awake, of course he was sleeping.

Virgil stirred, and his eyes opened.

Why was Virgil's mother sad? Where was Virgil's father?

"Oh," Rose sighed, sitting down at the edge of the bathtub, "I got left out of something that I would have liked to have been invited to. Your father went to help."

Virgil was sad for his mother. Virgil was sad to still be in the box. Could Virgil get out of the box? He was behaving.

"Yes, you are," Rose said, reaching in and picking him up. She held him in her arms, stroking his smooth and slippery scales. Sometimes things happened that put the events of her life in perspective. If nothing else, Virgil had hatched safely. He had been born healthy. That was a privilege that not all parents were given with their children.

Please be safe, Rose told Ophelia silently, even though she knew the thoughts would not reach at this distance. *Please be healthy. If anyone deserves that, they do.*

It wouldn't be right for them to lose two children. Nobody should even lose one.

Had Virgil's birth parents worried about losing their son this way? Had they ever realized that their son might, instead, lose them?

Virgil rubbed his tail on her arm as she stroked her hand down his back. He remembered his birth parents. He would show her one of their memories.

A memory from Virgil's father welled up, taking hold of her senses and gripping her in its all-absorption. Rose gasped as she recognized the familiarity of the scene.

He sneakily left the fire pit unscrubbed. He hated scrubbing the fire pit. Maybe his wife would do it for him.

Uh oh! His wife had noticed, and she was very annoyed.

It was his turn to scrub the fire pit, and he knew it! *And* he'd used one of her rocks to carve a picture into it! They were specimens, not pretty things!

It was a *pretty* specimen, and it would be much better as a carved rock than put boringly in a row in the vast rock collection cave!

Oh, now see what he did? The egg was whining that they were fighting again!

He could calm the baby. He was good at it. He'd show the baby a memory . . .

The memory faded, and Rose came to herself again.

"Was that a true memory?" she asked. "Or did you add to that one?"

Virgil didn't know what she meant. Did Virgil's mother like his old father's memory? He had forgotten all about it till now.

Rose bit her lip. That meant it was probably a true memory.

She'd almost forgotten that the reason Virgil had chosen them was because they resembled his birth parents so closely in personality. And that was the most in-depth memory she'd ever had of Virgil's birth father.

His birth parents had chosen one another. They'd had arguments, too. And yet, through that whole quarrel, there had been a strong sense of affection, of devotion to one another. A strong sense of this-is-the-right-match-for-me.

Of course they weren't the same people as Rose and Henry. They were only similar. And yet . . .

And yet . . . he loved her so much. And she felt the same about him.

Was that how Henry felt about her? Would she be capable of feeling that depth of emotion for him someday? Without jeopardizing who she was or what she wanted to be?

She wasn't sure. But she hoped . . . she hoped . . . she hoped it was possible.

Henry returned home late that night, which, fortunately, was many hours earlier than Rose had expected or feared.

"How did it go?" she asked, opening the door to let him and Mr. Teedle in. "Is Ophelia . . .?"

"The dragon's fine," Mr. Teedle said, removing his bowler hat. He rubbed one of his eyes, looking weary. "Once she got out, she was willing to eat with no troubles. It was getting out of the egg that was the difficulty for her. She was awfully weak."

Rose looked at Henry. "Did it help for you to be there?"

"Yes," Henry said. He held his hands cupped with the wrists together. "I showed them this, which helped her eat."

Rose felt a stab of annoyance. Mimicking a mouth with her hands had been her idea. *Deinonychus* parents had made crop milk for their infants inside their mouths, something humans obviously could not do, so pretending their hands were mouths had helped Virgil accept the uncomfortable situation at first.

Still, the important thing was that Henry had been able to help. And she was very glad the child was alive.

"I'm glad she's with her parents," Rose said aloud. "I'm glad she doesn't have to live in the zoo."

Mr. Teedle hesitated. "Well . . . I don't know about that. We'll be providing food for her for the first few weeks, because she'll need to be supervised carefully, but after that, it will be up to her parents to feed her. I'm not sure how they're going to afford it, frankly."

"They live in Harlem," Henry explained. "Not a wealthy neighborhood."

"That's not all," Mr. Teedle said grimly. "He's a musician. They both are. Alice sings, and Willie plays piano. And sometimes they do art on the side. Apparently that's how they make their money. I really don't see how they can support a child on that, much less a carnivore. That's just not something an artist can do!"

Henry's face had gone thunderous.

Oh, dear, Rose sighed. *He's taking that personally.*

"Artists are creative people," Henry snapped. "They're good at thinking up creative solutions. They'll manage."

"Of course they'll try," Mr. Teedle said, "but . . ."

"They'll manage!"

Mr. Teedle looked somewhat baffled at this vehemence.

"Thank you so much for giving Henry a ride back home," Rose said hastily. "It might be good for us to cut this visit short, as Virgil's already in bed and we don't want to wake him. Can we offer you some food before you head out again?"

CHAPTER 10
Special

It was only a week later that the invitation arrived. It was left on their doormat when Rose opened the door in the morning.

You are cordially invited to attend the debut performance of Ophelia Lawrence for an evening of dragon song. And then there was an illustration of a dragon hatchling, followed by the name and address of a Harlem vaudeville theater, as well as a time and tonight's date.

To say that Rose was shocked would be an understatement.

"What in the world!" she cried, reading it the first time.

Henry looked over her shoulder. He scanned it through, and then he started to laugh. "That's brilliant! They need a way to make money, so why not have people pay to see the baby? That's what the zoo would do, anyway!"

Virgil looked up from his breakfast of chicken mixed with raw egg and water. The zoo! He wanted to go to the zoo. Could he go to the zoo to see Violet now?

"No zoo for two weeks," Henry said. "That's your punishment for destroying the pram."

Virgil was VERY SAD! Virgil was going to shred his food and throw it all over the kitchen!

"Do that, and you won't get any more breakfast."

Virgil was sulking. Virgil was sullen. Virgil's parents hadn't let him go to the zoo for ages. Virgil wanted to smear food on the floor. Virgil was going to smear food on the floor. Virgil was smearing food all over the floor.

Henry went and fetched the tipped-over food bowl in one hand. With the other, he picked up the struggling dragon and carried the boy to the time-out box in the bathroom.

No! Virgil was sorry! Virgil didn't want to be in the box! Virgil was saaaaaaaaaad!

Henry shut the door to the bathroom just in time to partially muffle an earsplitting scream.

"If that's dragon song, I already hear enough of it," Rose announced.

Henry snorted with laughter. "I'm guessing it has to be better than that. Well, what do you think? Do you want to go?"

"I confess I'm curious," she admitted. "Even though I'm not sure how much the tickets cost."

For some reason, that made Henry chuckle. "You're never *not* curious. All right, then. We'll go."

Hours later, when they arrived at the vaudeville theater, the man taking tickets took one look at Virgil and shooed them in without taking their money, insisting that they had seats reserved for them inside. They soon discovered that this meant three parterre seats in the center of the front row. Four other seats were reserved around theirs.

"Why four people?" Henry wondered. "Who else is coming?"

"Relatives?" Rose asked.

"Of Alice and Willie's? Not likely." Henry gestured with his head. "I mean . . ."

Rose glanced back and saw what he meant. All the front rows were filled with white people. All the colored members of the audience were in the back rows.

"That hardly seems fair," she said.

"It is what it is," Henry shrugged, putting Virgil on his lap.

Five minutes later, a colored man ambled casually up to the front row and sat in one of the reserved seats next to them.

Rose gasped before she could stop herself. She glanced at the back row. She glanced at him. She glanced at Henry. She glanced back at the man.

The man grinned and held out his hand. "Name's Johnny. I'm Alice's big brother. Yeah, I'm sitting up front tonight. I'm the one who negotiated their pay, and I told the manager I had to sit in the front for their first performance, or no deal. He wasn't too happy about it, but he really wanted Ophy."

Henry shook the man's hand. "'Ophy'?" he repeated. "Is that Ophelia's nickname?"

The man grinned. "According to my sister, no, but according to me, yes. Sounds less stuck-up than Ophelia, right?"

Rose was spared the need to answer that she preferred the full name by the arrival of Violet's father.

"Harrison!" Henry called, waving. "Was one of these seats reserved for you?"

Harrison Jones veered over and joined them. "Apparently so." He stopped and gave the colored man an odd look.

"He's Alice's big brother," Henry explained. "He's sitting with us."

"Yeah, I guessed that," Harrison said, carefully sitting in the empty seat next to Rose rather than Johnny. "Why?"

"Because I am," Johnny said. "I'm not missing my niece's first performance. Only the people in the first few rows will be within range. And you can just get used to it, ma'am," he added to a scandalized-looking woman off to their left.

The woman got up and walked off in a huff.

"So who're the other two seats for?" Henry asked.

"Oh, Alice wanted all the dragon parents to get to be here for this."

Rose sucked in her breath in horror. *Bessie and Francis!*

Harrison smirked. "Those two? There's no way they're going to come. Much too good for vaudeville, I bet you."

Rose profoundly hoped that was true.

Fortunately, it seemed that Harrison's assessment was true. There was no sign of the wealthy couple as the first act started.

The first act featured a comedian whose jokes had Johnny and Harrison laughing uproariously. Next up was a woman in a beaded dress who sang in a high soprano. She was closely followed by a man and woman performing an Irish jig, then a man with a trained elephant.

Then came the fifth act.

A piano was pushed on stage, and Willie followed. He was the first colored person to walk on the stage so far tonight. Then Alice came out carrying a tiny yellow dragon.

She wore a long black sheathe of a dress, much simpler than the current fashion, and Ophelia wore what appeared to be an even simpler black tube of fabric, a fact which made Rose stare. Much as she believed in treating Virgil the same as a human infant, she would never have thought to put clothing on him. Doing so seemed faintly ridiculous.

There was a murmur of excitement across the audience. This was definitely what a lot of them had come to see.

Willie started playing, and the first thirty seconds of the song was an energetic ragtime melody that got Virgil so excited that he breathed fire straight in the air, causing screams of delight from the people behind them, who no doubt thought this was part of the show.

Rose fiercely remonstrated Virgil not to do that again in the quietest whisper she could lace with fury.

And then Alice started to sing.

Her singing voice was a reverberating alto that seemed to fill the whole room. It seemed nothing like the quiet voice she spoke with. And then even Rose's jolt of surprise at that was completely drowned out by Ophelia joining in.

The dragon's contribution was a small hum. In tune, but only one note, held out for long periods between her parents' interlacing melody and harmony. That could, perhaps, have been considered a song, but nothing special.

No, the special part was the colors.

In a wave around Ophelia, the room shifted around them, pulsing between normal colors and strange ones that Rose could not name. The pulsing started out in rhythm with the music and then rapidly lost the beat, which was probably not intended. But it hardly mattered.

In what seemed like no time at all, the song was over, and the spell broken.

Exclamations and chattering swept across the first few rows.

"Holy Hannah," Henry said, letting out an explosive breath. "She's a tetrachromat."

"A what?" Harrison and Johnny asked.

"It means she can see four colors," Henry said. "We can only see three. In this case, I think the fourth one is infrared."

"Is that normal for dragons?" Alice's brother asked.

"*No,*" Rose and Henry said simultaneously.

"How would you know?" Harrison Jones asked. "We've only ever met two dragons before."

"We know because we've seen the memories of hundreds of other dragons, courtesy of Violet and Virgil," Henry said. "None of them have shown colors like those. If Ophelia can do that . . . she's got a talent that's probably rare."

After a few minutes to let the murmurs from the crowd die down, the family of musicians began a second song. This time, Alice stepped off the stage and walked down to the audience, carrying Ophelia in her arms, so that the colors could reach more members of the audience than the first few rows.

It wasn't that it was a spectacular performance. Ophelia's contributions were rough, off the beat, and frequently sloppy. In addition, all she ever seemed to do was overlay her memories of this room on top of everybody else's, which was how she was making the colors seem to change back and forth for them.

Still, it was enough. It was sufficient.

This was definitely a performance that would pull in enough crowds to keep a hungry, small yellow dragon fed.

CHAPTER 11

Son

o, we have to," Henry insisted. "We have to tell them what they missed. They need to go so that they can see it before the show's booked solid."

"It was their own fault for being too snobbish to show up," Rose said acerbically. She had no wish to see the Baileys.

"We still have to tell them," Henry said. "It doesn't matter if you dislike them, Rose. Their son might very well be one of Virgil's friends in the future."

Rose held back her temper only because she knew it was true. Virgil and his games like "claw face" could not be trusted around human infants. If he was going to have any playmates in young childhood, and perhaps even afterwards, they would have to be dragons.

Of course she hoped that the other eight eggs waiting in the American Museum of Natural History would hatch at a rapid pace, but there was no guarantee of that. It was entirely possible that the only dragons awake in New York City in their generation would be Virgil, Violet, Philomel, and Ophelia. And if that happened, a continuing acquaintanceship with Bessie could not be avoided, no matter how much Rose might wish it.

"Oh, very well," Rose said testily. "We can drop in to tell them, if you insist."

It was strange how quick a walk it was from Harlem to 5th Avenue. The two seemed like they ought to be worlds apart, and yet in less than half an hour of walking, you could move from one to the other with ease.

As they reached the door to the Baileys' home, Rose flinched at the thought of deliberately initiating contact. But Henry was holding the handle of the wagon where Virgil was curled up sleeping, so she steeled herself and moved forward to knock.

Virgil jolted awake at the noise, and he let out a loud yowl. Then his eyes drooped, and he settled back into sleep.

A maid answered the door. "I'm afraid Mrs. Bailey is not at home," she said politely. "It might be best to come back later."

"Very well," Rose said, happy to take the offered reprieve.

"No, don't send them away!" a voice shouted from within the house.

A wild-eyed woman with disheveled hair came bolting down the stairs and pushed past the maid. She looked as if she had not slept in two days.

"How do you get him to eat on his own?!" Bessie screamed. "He won't take food from anybody but me! Not even Francis! He told the experts to go away, and he wouldn't stop screaming until they did! And he *bit* the nanny, and she *quit!*"

"Hang on," Rose said slowly. "Am I to understand that Philomel hatched?"

"*Yes!* And he's a nightmare! How do you fix it?!"

"Fix . . . the fact that he's hatched?" Rose asked blankly.

"YES! I LIKED HIM BETTER IN THE EGG!"

Henry stepped forward. "It sounds like you need some help. I'll volunteer," he said very politely. There was a slight shake in his voice. "Rose, if you would be so kind?"

He held out the handle of the wagon. She took it, not sure why he wanted to switch places. "You want me to carry Virgil's wagon inside?"

"Oh, no," Henry said with a gleam in his eyes, and she realized he was trying very hard to keep a straight face. "I can't imagine two fit-throwing infants in there would be helpful right now."

"No," Bessie said, wild-eyed. "No, no! Take him away!"

Rose could barely contain a straight face herself. Imagine Bessie asking her to leave!

She couldn't possibly be more delighted to surrender this hatching to Henry.

"Very well," Rose said demurely.

The wild-eyed harridan who bore little resemblance to the haughty gentlewoman who had plagued Rose over the past weeks stormed inside the house, ranting and yelling and howling about how terrible parenthood was, and why hadn't anybody ever told her that dragons were as bad as normal babies?!

The door slammed, and Rose waited until she was sure the woman was well out of earshot.

Then she doubled over and laughed and laughed and laughed.